For Charlie

First published 1998 by Walker Books Ltd
87 Vauxhall Walk, London SE11 5HJ

This edition published 2000

4 6 8 10 9 7 5

© 1998 Penny Dale

This book has been typeset in Stempel Schneidler.

Printed in China

British Library Cataloguing in Publication Data
A catalogue record for this book is
available from the British Library.

ISBN-13: 978-0-7445-7254-4
ISBN-10: 0-7445-7254-1

www.walkerbooks.co.uk

Ten Play
Hide-and-Seek

Penny Dale

WALKER BOOKS
AND SUBSIDIARIES
LONDON · BOSTON · SYDNEY · AUCKLAND

There were ten in the bed and the little one said,

"Let's play hide-and-seek!"

So the little one counted and the others went to hide.

"One, two, **three, four, five ...**

six, seven ... eight, nine and ...

ten!

Ready or not...

Here I come!" the little one said.

He looked under the bed and inside the drawer.

He went to the cupboard and opened the door.

BOO!

"Found you, Ted!" the little one said.

"That makes two of us!" the little one said.

"Now let's find the others."

They looked behind the curtains,

under the pillows,

inside the box of bricks.

They looked and they listened, and …

BOO! "Found you, Sheep!"

BOO! "Found you, Rabbit!"

BOO! "Found you, Zebra!"

"That makes five of us," the little one said.

"Now let's find the others."

They looked behind the coats,
under the table,

among the pots and the pans.
They looked and they looked, and …

BOO! "Found you, Hedgehog!"

BOO! "Found you, Bear!"

BOO! "Found you, Croc!"

BOO! "Found you, Nellie!"

"That makes nine," the little one said.
"Let me see. Someone's still missing...
Who can it be?"

"Not me,"
said Croc.

"Not me,"
said Nellie.

"Not me,"
said Hedgehog

"Not me," said Bear.

"Not me," said Zebra.

"Not me," said Rabbit.

"Not me," said Sheep.

"Not me," said Ted.

Then a teeny little voice squeaked . . .

"It's meeeeeee!"

"Found you, Mouse!" the little one said.

"Now we can **all** go to bed."

"Night-night, Ted. Night-night, Zebra.

Night-night, Rabbit, Bear and Sheep.

Night-night, Hedgehog. Night-night, Croc.

Night-night, Nellie, Mouse and me!"

"Night-night, everyone,"
the little one said.

Night-night, sleep tight,
ten in the bed.

TEN PLAY HIDE-AND-SEEK

Penny Dale says that *Ten Play Hide-and-Seek* came from noticing how very young children love peek-a-boo games. "I wanted to write a story around the idea of hide-and-seek, and to contrast the quiet, careful looking for clues in the pictures – a little paw, or a tiny eye – with the sudden "BOO!" as each animal is found," she explains. "The *Ten in the Bed* characters and their house seemed ideal for this, as there were so many of them and lots of places to hide!"

Penny Dale is one of this country's leading illustrators of children's books. For Walker she has illustrated the Martin Waddell stories *Once There Were Giants*; *When the Teddy Bears Came* and *Rosie's Babies* (shortlisted for the Kate Greenaway Medal and Winner of the Best Book for Babies Award), as well as her own stories, *Bet You Can't!*; *Ten in the Bed*; *Ten out of Bed*; *The Elephant Tree*; *All About Alice*; *Wake Up, Mr B!* (Commended for the Kate Greenaway Medal) and *Big Brother, Little Brother*.

Penny is married with a teenage daughter and lives in Caerleon, near Newport.

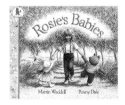 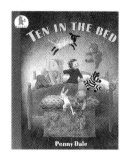 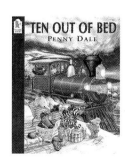  

FOR THE BEST CHILDREN'S BOOKS, LOOK FOR THE BEAR.